First
Facts®

SUPER SCARY STUFF

SUPER SCARY
MONSTERS

BY MEGAN COOLEY PETERSON

CAPSTONE PRESS
a capstone imprint

First Facts are published by Capstone Press,
1710 Roe Crest Drive, North Mankato, Minnesota 56003
www.mycapstone.com

Library of Congress Cataloging-in-Publication Data
Names: Peterson, Megan Cooley, author.
Title: Super scary monsters / by Megan Cooley Peterson.
Description: North Mankato, Minnesota : First Facts are published by Capstone
   Press, [2017] | Series: First facts. Super scary stuff | Includes
   bibliographical references and index.
Identifiers: LCCN 2015041214 | ISBN 9781515702771 (library binding) | ISBN
   9781515702818 (ebook pdf)
Subjects: LCSH: Monsters—Juvenile literature. | Animals, Mythical—Juvenile
   literature.
Classification: LCC GR825 .P49 2017 | DDC 001.944—dc23
LC record available at http://lccn.loc.gov/2015041214

Editorial Credits
Carrie Braulick Sheely, editor; Kyle Grenz, designer; Svetlana Zhurkin, media researcher;
   Katy LaVigne, production specialist

Photo Credits
Dreamstime: Jaime Pharr, 13 (back); Fortean Picture Library: William M. Rebsamen, 7 (left); Getty
Images: Ed Vebell, 9 (bottom); iStockphoto: Rich Legg, cover; Shutterstock: Alexlky, 11, DarkBird,
21, Denis Belitsky, 5, Fotokostic, 17, Lukasz Nowak, 9 (top), Neftali, 15 (inset), paintings, 15 (back),
Sergey Mironov, 1, Unholy Vault Designs, 7 (right); SuperStock: Pantheon, 13 (inset); Svetlana
Zhurkin, 19

Design Elements by Shutterstock

Printed and bound in China.
007702

TABLE OF CONTENTS

SCARY MONSTERS ALL AROUND

You're hiking in the woods. A twig snaps nearby. You turn to see a figure darting between the trees. What was it? For thousands of years, people have told monster stories. Some *legendary* creatures feed on blood. Others are half human and half animal. Monsters can be made-up. But others may be real. These scary creatures are whispered about in the dark. Are you ready to meet them?

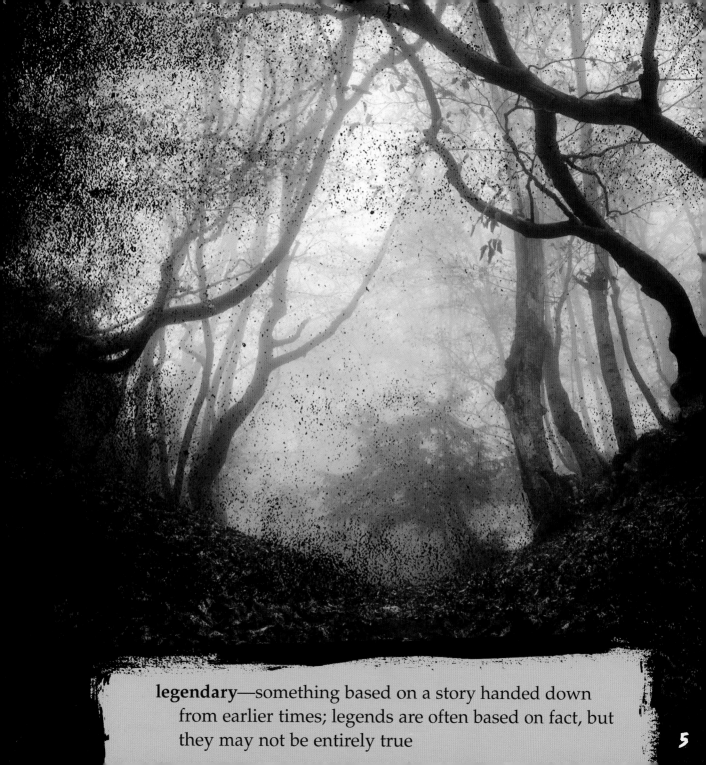

legendary—something based on a story handed down from earlier times; legends are often based on fact, but they may not be entirely true

A FLYING NIGHTMARE

Imagine riding in a car down a dark road. Suddenly a birdlike creature with glowing red eyes swoops down. You and the monster are face-to-face.

This monster was first reported near Point Pleasant, West Virginia, in 1966. People nicknamed it the Mothman. Some people say the Mothman is an *alien*. Others believe it's a large bird called a crane.

Creepy Cryptids

Some monsters, such as the Mothman, are called *cryptids*. Some people believe these monsters really exist. A few cryptids have turned out to be real animals. People once believed in a cryptid called the kraken. It was said to pull ships underwater. Researchers now believe this animal was the giant squid.

alien—a creature not from Earth
cryptid—a creature whose existence has not been proven by science

MONSTER IN THE MOUNTAINS

The snowy Himalayas in Asia may hold a hairy secret. People have spotted an apelike creature called the yeti in the mountains for years. Some reports say the yeti has white fur. Others say its fur is dark. Many people think the yeti is a kind of ape that hasn't been discovered. Reports say the yeti stands 8 feet (2.4 meters) tall or more. It is said to weigh about 300 pounds (136 kilograms).

The word *yeti* comes from the **Sherpa** phrase "yet-teh." The word has many meanings, including "little manlike animal" and "animal of rocky places."

Sherpa—a member of a group of Tibetan people living in the Himalayas in eastern Nepal; Sherpas are known for helping mountain climbers

A HAIRY BLOODSUCKER

Move over, Count Dracula. There's a new bloodsucking monster on the hunt—the chupacabra. According to legend, this doglike cryptid sucks the blood of small animals. It hunts in Central America and the southern United States. Reports say it has glowing eyes and long, sharp claws. A terrible smell follows wherever it goes. *Skeptics* say the chupacabra is a dog or coyote with a skin disease.

skeptic—a person who questions things that other people believe in

The word *chupacabra* means "goat sucker" in Spanish.

A DEADLY DRAGON

According to *folklore*, a hideous dragon once lived in the River Wear in England. Called the Lambton Worm, slimy skin covered its body. It had no legs or wings. Its breath killed anyone who smelled it. This monster snatched up animals and people with its sharp teeth. At night the dragon wrapped its huge body around a hill to sleep.

folklore—ideas or stories that are not true but that many people have heard

SWAMP BEAST

Beware of the swamps and lakes of Australia. The bunyip is said to call these waters home. Reports about the creature's looks vary. Some say it has the head of an *emu* or dog with a hairy body. The bunyip eats anyone who dares to enter its watery home. But even people on land aren't safe. At night this monster leaves the water. It gobbles up everyone in sight.

The *Aborigines* of Australia first described the bunyip. These people arrived in Australia about 50,000 years ago.

A BUNYIP OF ABORIGINAL LEGEND

emu—a large, flightless Australian bird that runs fast
Aborigine—one of the native peoples of Australia whose ancestors lived there before Europeans arrived

BULL-HEADED MONSTER

The minotaur was one of the scariest monsters from ancient Greek *myths*. It had the head of a bull. Its body was human. This beast used razor-sharp teeth and horns to attack its victims.

The minotaur lived in a *labyrinth*. It hungered for only one thing—human flesh. Anyone caught in its mazelike home was eaten alive.

myth—a story told by people in ancient times; myths often tried to explain natural events
labyrinth—a maze of winding passages

According to the myth, the Greek hero Theseus killed the minotaur.

THE FLYING HEAD

According to Malaysian folklore, a bloodsucking monster lives in plain sight. During the day the Penanggalan looks like a woman. But at night its head detaches from its body. Guts dangle from this monster's head as it flies around. It hungers for human blood.

Types of Vampires

Every *culture* has its own vampire legend. In some stories, vampires look like regular humans. In others vampires are balls of fiery blue light. In most legends vampires drink human blood.

culture—a people's way of life, ideas, art, customs, and traditions

A WATERY END

English folklore says the murky ponds of northern England hide a scary monster. A woman with green skin, hair, and teeth hides beneath the surface. She is called Jenny Greenteeth. This monster waits for children to come near. She then uses her long arms and sharp nails to drag them to their doom.

The Jenny Greenteeth story isn't real. But some people think the yeti and other monsters might exist. Real or not, it's fun to tell stories about creepy monsters among us.

Jenny Greenteeth is sometimes called Wicked Jenny.

GLOSSARY

Aborigine (ab-uh-RIJ-uh-nee)—one of the native peoples of Australia whose ancestors lived there before Europeans arrived

alien (AY-lee-uhn)—a creature not from Earth

cryptid (KRIP-tihd)—a creature whose existence has not been proven by science

culture (KUHL-chuhr)—a people's way of life, ideas, art, customs, and traditions

emu (E-myu)—a large, flightless Australian bird that runs fast

folklore (FOK-lor)—ideas or stories that are not true but that many people have heard

labyrinth (LAB-uh-rynth)—a maze of winding passages

legendary (LEJ-uhnd)—something based on a story handed down from earlier times; legends are often based on fact, but they may not be entirely true

myth (MITH)—a story told by people in ancient times; myths often tried to explain natural events

Sherpa (SHER-puh)—a member of a group of Tibetan people living in the Himalayas in eastern Nepal; Sherpas are known for helping mountain climbers

skeptic (SKEP-tik)—a person who questions things that other people believe in

victim (VIK-tuhm)—a person who is hurt, killed, or made to suffer

READ MORE

Burgan, Michael. *The Unsolved Mystery of Bigfoot.* Unexplained Mysteries. North Mankato, Minn.: Capstone, 2013.

Roberts, Steven. *Chupacabras!* Jr. Graphic Monster Stories. New York: PowerKids Press, 2013.

Weakland, Mark. *Scooby-Doo! and the Truth Behind Vampires.* Unmasking Monsters with Scooby-Doo! North Mankato, Minn.: Capstone, 2015.

INTERNET SITES

FactHound offers a safe, fun way to find Internet sites related to this book. All of the sites on FactHound have been researched by our staff.

Here's all you do:

Visit *www.facthound.com*

Type in this code: 9781515702771

INDEX

DED